SWORD OF THE SAMURAI

Adventure Stories from Japan

SWORD OF THE

ERIC A. KIMMEL

SAMURAI

Adventure Stories from Japan

BROWNDEER PRESS

HARCOURT BRACE & COMPANY

San Diego   New York   London

Browndeer Press is a registered trademark of Harcourt Brace & Company.

Library of Congress Cataloging-in-Publication Data
Kimmel, Eric A.
Sword of the samurai: adventure stories from Japan/Eric A. Kimmel.
p. cm.
"Browndeer Press."
Includes bibliographical references.
Summary: Eleven short stories about samurai warriors, their way of life,
courage, wit, and foolishness.
ISBN 0-15-201985-5
1. Children's stories, American.   2. Samurai—Juvenile fiction.
[1. Samurai—Fiction.   2. Japan—Fiction.   3. Short stories.]   I. Title.
PZ7.K5648Sw   1999
[Fic]—dc21   98-16633

Text set in Galliard
Designed by Camilla Filancia
First edition   F E D C B A

Printed in the United States of America

For the children and teachers
of the American School
in Japan
—E. A. K.

Contents

SWORD OF THE SAMURAI

Adventure Stories from Japan

KNIGHTS OF
OLD JAPAN

MOST PEOPLE have heard exciting stories about King Arthur and the knights of the Round Table. Knights were the fighting men of Europe's Middle Ages who rode into battle dressed in suits of elaborate armor.

The samurai were the knights of old Japan. They, too, wore elaborate armor and carried swords, which are among the most beautiful ever made. The European knight's values and conduct were shaped by his Christian faith. In a similar way, the samurai's outlook and character were molded by Shintoism and Buddhism, Japan's two major religions. Bushido, the warrior's code, emphasized the values of humility, honor, and loyalty to one's master, living in harmony with nature, self-control, and surprisingly, nonviolence. The great samurai masters never drew their swords unless absolutely necessary.

The Middle Ages in Europe lasted about one thousand years, beginning in the fifth century A.D. and ending in the fifteenth. Japan's medieval period began at about the same time but lasted two hundred years longer. The samurai way of life began drawing to a close in the seventeenth century, when powerful military leaders called shoguns defeated rival factions and broke up their armies, and brought the country under the authority of one ruler. The age of the fighting samurai ended forever in the nineteenth century, when the emperor of Japan and his supporters broke the shoguns' power, took back control of the government, and began the process of transforming Japan into a modern nation. Samurai ideals are still revered in Japan and remain important guides to personal conduct in politics, business, and daily life. They are also the foundation for the modern martial arts.

DŌHAKU'S
HEAD

The Japanese, like most peoples of the world, have a tradition of telling tall tales. A story begins with an ordinary incident, to which increasingly unlikely episodes are added. The storyteller insists that the tale is entirely true.

This story is true. It has been documented.

A SAMURAI NAMED Dōhaku was once traveling through a forest when two *rōnin* suddenly attacked him. Before he could draw his sword, they cut off his head.

A lesser man would have died on the spot. But Dōhaku was a samurai of the old school. Even though his head was gone, he was still unwilling to admit defeat. He was also extremely angry to have been taken by surprise.

Dōhaku drew his sword and attacked the *rōnin* so furiously that they threw down their weapons and fled. Having driven off his enemies, Dōhaku got down on his knees and began looking for his head.

"I'm over here! Farther to the left!" his head cried out.

Dōhaku finally found his head beneath a bush. He picked it up, washed it off in a stream, tucked it under his arm, and carried it home.

Dōhaku's wife screamed when her husband came walking through the door holding his head in his hands.

"Don't make so much noise," Dōhaku's head said. "There's no time to waste. Run and fetch the doctor. Quick!"

The doctor arrived moments later. After examining the patient, he said, "This is a most unusual case. I cannot guarantee that Dōhaku-san will recover, but I will do what I can." He asked the head, "Do you feel any pain?"

"None whatsoever! Even my old wounds no longer bother me. I cannot feel them at all."

"Understandable," the doctor said. "But I will try to reattach you. You cannot go about the village like this. It would frighten the children."

The doctor painted Dōhaku's neck with a

special glue made from pine resin, garlic oil, and healing herbs. He put Dōhaku's head back on his shoulders. Then he wound a silk cord tightly around Dōhaku's neck to hold the head in place. After making Dōhaku sit in an empty rice bin, he buried him in rice, so that only his topknot showed.

"Stay there and don't move," the doctor said.

Three days later the doctor uncovered Dōhaku's face. "How do you feel?" he asked.

"Fine!" Dōhaku said.

The doctor covered him up.

Three days later the doctor asked again, "How do you feel?"

"Perfectly well!" said Dōhaku.

The doctor covered him up again.

Three days after that, the doctor dug away the rice and asked again, "Well, how do you feel now?"

"I feel terrible!" Dōhaku groaned. "I'm hungry. I'm thirsty. My back aches. My knees are torturing me. My whole body feels as if it is on fire. How much longer must I endure this sitting?"

"You don't have to endure it at all," the doctor said. "Get up. You are cured."

Dōhaku's wife helped her husband to his feet. The doctor unwound the silk cord from around the samurai's neck.

Dōhaku moved his head from side to side. "My head is back on again!" he exclaimed, extremely pleased.

It is often said that the samurai of recent times are nothing like the samurai of ages past.

Neither are the doctors.

THE SAMURAI
AND THE DRAGON

*Traditional Japanese society
emphasized the importance of the group
over the interests of the individual. All
samurai had a particular place in their
family, in their clan, and in their lord's
household. Consequently, samurai
dismissed from their lord's service suffered
more than disgrace. They lost their "place."
In the eyes of their fellow samurai, they
vanished. Unless they could find another
lord, they were doomed to a marginal
existence, surviving as best they could on
society's fringes.*

THERE WAS ONCE a samurai named Hido who was strong and brave and skilled in the use of all types of weapons. Yet, despite his skill and courage, Hido lacked luck. He always found himself on the losing side. Every master he served was defeated. Every battle he fought was lost. None of this was Hido's fault. Could he be blamed if the enemy's numbers were too great, if cowardly soldiers ran away, if the plan of attack was flawed and the battlefield poorly chosen? Hido always strived to do his best. Yet, after a while, people began saying, "Hido brings bad luck. Everyone he fights for loses."

As a result, no lord would employ Hido. No

general would take him into his service. No officer wanted to have an unlucky samurai in his ranks. Hido wandered from castle to castle seeking work, but he always met the same answer: "Hido-san, you are a brave samurai. I would like to hire you, but I fear the bad luck you bring."

Hido soon found himself ragged and penniless. He had to sell his armor to buy food. Eventually all he had left were his sword, his bow, and three arrows.

"What can I do?" Hido asked himself. "I have only two choices, and neither one is good. If I take up a trade or open a shop, I will lose my samurai rank. If I become a *rōnin*—a masterless samurai who lives by robbing others—I will lose my self-respect."

He decided to keep trying a little longer. Surely there was a master somewhere who would not let a flock of silly rumors prevent him from hiring a loyal, brave samurai.

Hido walked for a long time, until he came to a lake. In the distance, he saw a boat drawn up on shore. "I will use that boat to get to the other side," Hido said to himself.

When he reached the boat, he saw that it was guarded by a giant serpent. The snake's body was as thick as Hido's thigh. Its head was as large as the boat, while its tail extended so far beneath the waters of the lake that Hido could not see where it ended.

Hido drew his sword, approaching cautiously. The snake's eyes remained open, but the creature did not move. Hido remembered hearing that snakes, like fish, sleep with their eyes open. *Maybe it is asleep*, he thought. *As long as it does not attack me, I will do it no harm.*

Hido sheathed his sword and carefully stepped over the snake. He pushed the boat away from shore, got in, and began to row.

The boat moved swiftly at first. As the shoreline receded, the boat went more and more slowly. By the time Hido reached the middle of the lake, it would not move at all, no matter how hard he rowed.

"This is strange," said Hido to himself.

"Not strange at all!" a voice replied. Hido turned around. Sitting in the bow of the boat was an old gentleman dressed in the clothes of ancient times.

"Who are you?" Hido asked.

"We have met before," the gentleman answered. "I was the snake you stepped over. I am also the king of the Realm Below the Waters."

"Where is that?"

"At the bottom of this lake, beneath a crystal dome. What is your name?"

"My name is Hido. What do you want of me?"

"If you wish, I would like you to become one of my samurai."

"Are you sure you want that? No other lord will hire me. They all say I am unlucky."

"They can say what they like. What I care about most is that you are brave and clever. I have lain in my serpent shape beside this boat for a long time. No other samurai has had the courage or the wit to step over me. They all either run away or draw their swords and attack. You, on the other hand, did not turn from danger. Nor did you start a fight when there was an easier way to achieve your goal. When you stepped over me, I knew you had the qualities of an exceptional samurai. You are the man I am looking for."

Hido was doubtful. "Why do you need me so badly? Surely you must have many samurai in your service."

"Not as many as I once had." The king sighed. "It is all because of that cursed dragon."

"What dragon?"

The king then told Hido this story: "Many years ago I quarreled with a demon. Seeking revenge, the demon sent a mighty dragon to trouble my kingdom. Every night when the moon is full, this dragon plunges into the lake. He breaks through the crystal dome and seizes as many of my people as he can. My samurai are very brave. They have tried hard to fight him. But the dragon's body is covered with iron scales. Swords and arrows bounce off him. The dragon has devoured my bravest samurai. I have hardly any left."

"The moon will be full tonight," said Hido. "I accept your offer. I would like to try my skill against this dragon."

"Come with me."

The king of the Realm Below the Waters took Hido's hand. Together they leaped into the lake. Down, down, down they sank, until they arrived at the lake bottom. There, to his amazement, Hido saw a gigantic crystal dome covering a vast city. They entered through a gate made from one solid pearl.

The king led Hido to his palace, where they ate and drank until the sun went down. Looking up, they saw the light of the full moon shining upon the lake's surface.

"The dragon will be here in a little while,"

the king said. "How do you propose to fight him? Will you need a suit of armor?"

"Armor is no use against a dragon," Hido said. "My victory will depend on accuracy and speed. I have three arrows in my quiver. That should be enough."

The king frowned. "The dragon is mightier than you realize. You will need at least a hundred arrows to bring him down."

"Not so," said Hido. "Once the dragon attacks, I will only have time to shoot three arrows. If they fail to stop him, a thousand more won't do me any good."

Suddenly a terrible roar shook the palace. The walls and floor swayed, as if seized by an earthquake.

"The dragon is coming!" the king cried.

Hido picked up his bow and arrows.

The dome overhead shattered as the dragon battered his way into the city. People fled through the flooded streets, screaming as they attempted to escape both the dragon and the rising water.

The king's few samurai formed ranks and prepared to fight.

"Leave him to me!" Hido shouted. Fitting an arrow to his bowstring, he shot at the huge dragon . . . and missed!

Hido cursed his poor aim. "I truly am unlucky! How could anyone miss a target as big as that?" He fitted a second arrow to his bow as the dragon charged. It bounced off the iron scales.

With the dragon nearly upon him, Hido took out his third and last arrow. He spit on the arrowhead three times for luck. He aimed between the dragon's eyes and released the bowstring.

The dragon bellowed with rage. It took three steps forward, then fell with a crash.

Hido drew his sword and cut off the dragon's head.

The king and all the people of the Realm Below the Waters hailed Hido as a hero.

"How did you know that human spit is

deadly poison to dragons and demons?" the king asked. "I never told you that."

"I did not know. I was lucky," Hido said.

And from that day on, he was.

THE COWARD

*Samurai were elite warriors who had
studied the martial arts since childhood.
In contrast, the common soldiers who
fought in the ranks were half-trained
farmers taken from their homes. Their
officers had little respect for them, and the
enemy usually showed them no mercy.
These men had little to look forward to, in
either victory or defeat, except the hope of
surviving and being allowed to return
home one day.*

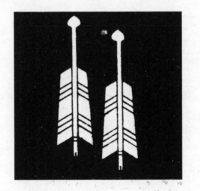

TWO OFFICERS once brought a common soldier before Lord Raikō for judgment. "What has he done?" Lord Raikō asked.

"This man is a coward. He ran away during battle," the officers replied.

"What shall we do with him?" Lord Raikō asked his lieutenant, Urabe no Suetake.

Suetake answered at once. "Cowards must die. Kill him!"

The soldier fell to his knees. "Have pity on me. I can't help being afraid. I'm a farmer, not a soldier. I was dragged from my home and forced to fight."

"What soldier isn't afraid?" Lord Raikō

answered. "If we accepted your excuse, we would have no army at all."

Suetake drew his sword. "Enough of this chatter. Let me cut off his head."

The soldier spoke suddenly. "I am sorry your eyesight is not as keen as it once was."

Suetake paused. "What do you mean? My eyesight is fine."

"Everyone knows that Urabe no Suetake is the greatest archer in Japan," the soldier said. "I have heard that you once shot a needle hanging from a thread as you rode by on horseback. Is that true?"

"Of course it's true! I demonstrated that feat five years ago in Kyoto, at the archery competition at the Rengeoin temple. And I can do it again! There is nothing wrong with my eyesight. Or my aim."

"Then why kill me with a sword? What is the challenge in that? Would you not prefer to use me as a living target? I would not mind dying so much if I knew I had the honor of being brought down by an arrow from Urabe no Suetake's bow."

Suetake was flattered. "If you feel that way, let's make this a real contest," he suggested. "Do you see the tree standing at the edge of this field? I estimate it is about a thousand yards away. You are to run toward it. If you manage to live long enough to reach the tree, I will ask Lord Raikō to spare your life."

Lord Raikō agreed. "I will do more than that. I will give you a purse of gold and release you from the army."

"Your lordships are most generous. I accept the challenge," the soldier said.

Suetake strung his bow. "All you have to do is get across the field to that tree." Then he whispered to Lord Raikō, "This will be easier than shooting rabbits."

Lord Raikō raised his fan as Suetake fitted an arrow to the bowstring. *"Go!"*

The soldier began running. The rest of the army gathered to watch. Soldiers and officers placed bets on how far the man would get before Suetake shot him down. No one thought he would last long enough to reach the middle of the field.

Suetake raised his bow. He took careful aim, released the bowstring, . . . and missed! The arrow flew to the right as the soldier ran on.

"How could I have missed such an easy shot?" Suetake asked himself. "There must have been a sudden gust of wind." He fitted another arrow to his bowstring, aimed again, . . . and missed! This time the arrow went to the left.

Suetake shot two quiverfuls of arrows at the soldier. He missed every time. Not a single arrow came close!

By now the soldier had reached the end of the field. He flung his arms around the tree.

"Well done!" Lord Raikō called to him. "Come back here and claim your reward."

The soldier walked back across the field.

Suetake confronted him, red-faced with anger. "What is your secret? What spell did you cast on me to cause my arrows to miss? Did you learn this trick from a wizard?"

"No, my lord. I used no spells and no tricks," the soldier replied. "Only a secret I learned from a rabbit."

"A rabbit?" Lord Raikō chuckled. "Explain this to us."

The soldier began. "One summer when I was a boy, a rabbit invaded our vegetable patch. None of our snares worked. He could outrun all our dogs. One night my father sent me out with a bow and arrow, telling me to shoot the rabbit when he appeared. I was a good shot; much better than my brothers. I saw the rabbit many times, yet I never could hit him. At last I realized why.

"There is a brief moment between the time when the archer releases the bowstring and the instant the arrow strikes its mark. The rabbit listened for the twang of my bowstring. As soon as he heard it, he jumped aside. My arrow went exactly where I aimed it, but the rabbit was no longer there."

He turned to Suetake. "I knew you would aim for the middle of my back. As I ran, I listened for the bowstring. The instant I heard it, I jumped aside. Your arrows passed without touching me."

"How clever of that rabbit! Be grateful. You owe your life to him," Lord Raikō told the soldier. "I grant you a full pardon. Take this purse and these documents. They are your release from the army. You are free to go home."

"He learned something from a rabbit, and I learned something from a coward," Suetake sneered.

"Don't say that," Lord Raikō said. "No person who volunteers to run a thousand yards across an open field while Urabe no Suetake shoots arrows at him can ever be called a coward. He was just not a very good soldier."

MATAJURO'S TRAINING

Samurai began military training at an early age. They practiced for hours each day under the guidance of their sensei, a highly respected teacher of the martial arts. The senseis taught swordsmanship and the use of weapons. More important, they instilled in their students the samurai virtues of courage, loyalty, endurance, patience, humility, hard work, and self-control. These qualities are still honored in Japan today and are taught in martial arts academies—dojos—throughout the world.

YAGYU MATAJURO, the son of a samurai family, showed skill with the sword at an early age. However, he was lazy. He refused to practice or exercise. While his brothers trained hard with their *sensei*, Matajuro would sneak out of the dojo to go fishing. Threats and punishment did no good. Matajuro's father scolded him before the entire clan—a terrible humiliation. Matajuro didn't care. The day arrived when he refused to do anything. He insulted his *sensei* and fought with his brothers when they tried to make him behave.

His father, extremely angry, told Matajuro to gather his belongings. "You come from a samurai family, but you have shown yourself unworthy. I will not tolerate your laziness and disrespect. You are my son no more. Get out!''

Matajuro had to leave home. He was cold and hungry. Sometimes a kind farmer would give him a bit of rice and allow him to sleep in his barn. But most often the country people, who once had bowed to him with respect, chased him away.

''Begone, you lazy boy! You were a samurai's son once, but no longer. You didn't want to work or study. How does it feel now, having to beg for food?''

Matajuro soon realized what a terrible mistake he had made. He vowed to change his ways. He went to his father and begged to be taken back.

''I have learned my lesson,'' he pleaded. ''I promise to work hard from now on. I will be lazy and disrespectful no longer.''

His father refused to listen. ''You had your opportunity to make something of yourself. I warned you many times not to waste it. You ignored me; now I ignore you. Maybe you can find someone to teach you the way of the samurai, but it will not be me."

Matajuro had to leave home again, this time for good. He became a vagabond, wandering around the countryside, hoping one day to find a *sensei* who would accept him as a pupil. Unfortunately, every *sensei* he spoke to already knew his story.

"I want students who work hard and show respect," each said. "Your own father threw you out. Why should I take you in?"

One day Matajuro learned of a *sensei* named Banzo, a monk who lived in a hut near the Kumano Machi Shrine. He was known to be kind and patient with his students. Matajuro went to see him. He kneeled at the *sensei*'s door and begged to be accepted as his pupil.

Banzo stepped over the boy as if he wasn't there, but Matajuro was not ready to give up. He knew this was his last chance. He lay in the doorway for a month, hoping that the *sensei* would notice him.

Banzo paid no attention at all. He stepped over Matajuro as he went in and out of his hut.

But one day Banzo asked, "What are you doing here, boy? Why are you lying in my doorway?"

"I want to be a swordsman, Master. Please accept me as your pupil. I promise to work hard, day and night. Don't turn me away. Teach me how to be a samurai."

Banzo sighed. "All right. Come in."

Matajuro lived with Banzo for the next three years. He cooked the rice, washed the clothes, swept the floor, gathered the firewood. The *sensei* did not talk to him at all, except to tell him what to do. As for learning swordsmanship, Matajuro never even saw a sword.

Matajuro began to grow impatient. *I am not learning to be a samurai,* he thought. *I am only a servant. All I do is cook and clean. If the* sensei *is not going to teach me anything, perhaps I should move on.*

He spoke to Banzo the next day. "Master, I have been here three years. When are you going to teach me something about swordsmanship?"

"Oh," said Banzo. "So you want to learn swordsmanship? Very well." He opened a chest and tossed Matajuro a wooden sword. "Practice with this."

Matajuro felt better, but not for long. Though in his spare moments he practiced the few exercises he remembered from his father's house, his *sensei* did not criticize or correct him. Banzo did not attempt to teach him anything. He ignored Matajuro, just as before.

One night, while Matajuro lay asleep, a heavy object whacked him across the shoulders. He cried out in pain. Opening his eyes, he saw Banzo standing over him, wielding a wooden sword. *Whack!* The sword came down again.

"Master! Why are you hitting me?" Matajuro cried.

"If you don't like being hit, defend yourself!" Banzo struck him again.

"I can't! My sword is hanging on the wall."

"Why is it there?"

Banzo beat Matajuro mercilessly with the

wooden sword. Every time the boy tried to get up, the *sensei* knocked him down.

After that, Matajuro made sure to sleep with his sword at his side. He carried it with him during the day, because he never knew when Banzo might attack him. When he least expected it—*whack!*—there came a blow across his head, legs, or shoulders.

Slowly, Matajuro learned to defend himself. He practiced harder and harder, developing lightning reflexes and split-second timing. After a while he could sense when an attack was about to come. Banzo seldom caught him off guard. This was vital, because they practiced with real swords now.

One day Matajuro was cooking rice when Banzo attacked without warning. Matajuro was ready. He didn't bother to draw his sword. Holding the pot's iron lid in his left hand, he parried his *sensei*'s thrusts while continuing to stir the rice with his right. When the rice was done, he filled a bowl and offered it to Banzo with a bow.

"Master, here is your dinner."

Banzo threw down his sword and embraced him. "You are ready, Matajuro. You have mastered the swordsman's art completely. There is nothing left for you to learn."

"Thank you for teaching me," Matajuro said.

Banzo shrugged. "You are mistaken. I did not teach you anything. The skills you possess were always yours. They were inside you from the beginning. I merely showed you how to let them out."

Banzo presented Matajuro with a fine sword on the day the boy left the Kumano Machi Shrine to return to his family. Matajuro became a famous samurai. His family was proud of him.

Matajuro never saw his *sensei* again, but he never forgot the lesson Banzo had taught him: Before one can master any art, one must first learn to master oneself.

THE OXCART

Old Japan had strict rules governing how people of all classes should behave. Highborn women were not allowed to have any contact with commoners. They could travel only in two-wheeled oxcarts. Small windows and heavy curtains hid the passengers from unwelcome stares. Although these carts were beautifully furnished and decorated, they were cramped, poorly ventilated, and extremely uncomfortable to ride in. The oxcarts were reserved for women. No male samurai could ride in one. If he did and was caught, he faced severe punishment, possibly even the loss of his samurai status. The three samurai in this story tried to cut corners. They learned a well-deserved lesson.

THE GOVERNOR of Settsu had three outstanding samurai in his service. Their names were Taira no Hidemichi, Taira no Suetake, and Sakata no Kintoki. Once in late fall, when the time of the Kamo festival was approaching, the three samurai wanted to go to Murasakino to watch the procession. They looked forward to seeing the beautiful shrines pulled through the streets on wagons while the great *taiko* drums filled the air with their pounding rhythm.

"How will we get to Murasakino?" Hidemichi asked.

"We'll ride our horses," Suetake suggested.

"That's not a good idea," said Kintoki. "The

streets in Murasakino are going to be crowded. Our horses are trained for war. Once they find themselves in the middle of those crowds, they'll think they're on a battlefield. They'll start kicking and plunging. Someone's bound to get hurt, and it will be our fault. The governor will be very angry with us."

"Then we'll walk," said Hidemichi.

"Three samurai walking along on foot, like common peasants? We'd be disgraced," Suetake replied.

"We could cover our faces so no one would know who we are," Kintoki suggested.

Hidemichi argued against that idea. "The city guards would take us for bandits. We'd end up in jail, and the governor would have to get us out. Even if we could go by foot, it's a long walk to Murasakino and back. I don't want to do it."

"Neither do we," Kintoki and Suetake agreed.

"If we can't walk or ride, how will we get there?" Suetake asked.

"I have an idea," Kintoki said. "We'll go in an oxcart."

"What? A farmer's wagon?"

"No! I mean the kind of closed oxcart that the wives and daughters of highborn nobles ride in."

"Is that a good idea?" Hidemichi asked. "Samurai are warriors. We aren't allowed to ride in carts or wagons. If anyone sees us, we'll be disgraced."

"Nobody will see us," Kintoki assured him. "These oxcarts are completely enclosed. The windows are covered with heavy curtains so no one can see inside."

"How will we get one?" Suetake asked. "Three samurai can't hire an oxcart without the whole town learning about it."

"I've thought of that already," said Kintoki. "My sister is lady-in-waiting to the governor's wife. The governor has plenty of oxcarts. Some are hardly ever used. My sister can arrange for us to borrow one. We'll walk along beside it on the way through town, pretending we're an escort. When no one is looking, we'll get in and ride all the way to Murasakino. Our servant, Akira, will lead the ox while we travel in comfort."

The plan worked perfectly—except for one unforeseen difficulty. The three samurai had never traveled in an oxcart. Although the vehicle looked elegant, it had no springs. Every bump in the road bounced them around like grains of rice pounded in a mortar. And there were many, many bumps, holes, and gullies along the way to Murasakino.

They had hardly gone a mile when Suetake turned pale. "I feel sick. I think I'm going to throw up," he said. "Hurry! Open the door! Let me out!"

Kintoki and Hidemichi grabbed him. "You can't go out! The road is full of people. If they see us riding in this oxcart, we'll be in trouble!"

"I can't help it!" Suetake moaned. "You have to let me out. I'm going to be—"

Poor Suetake threw up all over the oxcart. Like a seasick traveler, he couldn't stop vomiting, even when his stomach was empty. He lay helpless on the floor, moaning and coughing.

Hidemichi turned pale. "What a terrible stench! Open the curtains, Kintoki, or I'll be sick, too!"

"I can't open the curtains! No one must see us in here!" said Kintoki.

"Then I am going to be sick with Suetake!" Hidemichi clutched his stomach and threw up, too. Within minutes Kintoki joined him. The three samurai lay in a heap, vomiting on each other, groaning in misery.

The people on the road to Murasakino heard terrible groans coming from the oxcart. "What is going on in there?" they asked Akira, the samurais' servant. "It sounds as if someone is dying. Open the door! The people inside need help."

"Don't touch that door!" Akira blurted out. He could not allow his masters to be discovered riding in a women's oxcart. "The governor's aunt is inside. She was suddenly stricken with a terrible disease. Oozing sores broke out all over her body. The doctors can't help her. She is going to the temple in Murasakino to pray for a cure. No one must go near that cart. She might have the plague."

Needless to say, no one approached the cart again. The opposite happened. People on the road ran away when they saw the oxcart coming. It continued on to Murasakino, lurching back and forth on the bumpy road, with the three miserable samurai tumbling around inside it.

At last the cart stopped. "Masters, we are here. We've reached the outskirts of Murasakino," Akira whispered. He waited for a reply but heard nothing. Finally he said, "I'm going to find a pasture for the ox. Then I'm going to watch the procession. Come quickly. It will be starting soon."

Akira unhitched the ox and led it away.

When he returned hours later, he found the ox-cart door still shut, with no sign that his masters had ever emerged. Fearing they might be dead, Akira opened the door and peeped inside.

He saw the three samurai lying in a heap, too weak to stand or even groan. Akira lifted them out of the cart, one by one. "Masters, I am so sorry. I did not know you were so ill. Have you been here the whole time? Didn't you go to the festival?"

"How could we?" Kintoki answered. "We were so sick we could hardly lift our heads."

"How stupid we were to ride in that cart!" Suetake exclaimed.

Hidemichi agreed. "We suffered for nothing. We missed the whole festival."

Akira ran to an inn down the road. He returned with hot water, new clothes, and a kettle of hot soup. The samurai felt better after cleaning themselves and eating.

"Let's go home," Kintoki said, disgusted.

"Not in that cart," said Hidemichi and

Suetake. "We'll walk beside it. We'll pretend we're an escort."

The three samurai walked all the way back to Settsu. It took a long time to get there. They walked slowly, holding their stomachs, dragging their swords in the dust.

Kintoki's sister was waiting for them. "Where have you been? I was expecting you hours ago. Why do you look so pale? Why does the cart smell so bad?"

"You're lucky we brought it back at all. This cart should be burned!" Kintoki told her.

"The horrid vehicle nearly killed us!" Hidemichi added.

"I'd rather face slow death by torture than ride in an oxcart again!" said Suetake.

Kintoki's sister began to laugh. "You samurai are always telling your wives and sisters how tough you are! You only went to Murasakino. One short ride in an oxcart and you come back looking like corpses. We women are tougher than you! We ride in these carts all the time. Ha, ha, ha!"

Kintoki, Suetake, and Hidemichi slunk away without a word.

The three samurai had long, distinguished careers. Kintoki climbed the walls of an enemy castle and opened the gate, all by himself. Suetake stood alone in the middle of a bridge and fought off an attacking army. Hidemichi, after losing his sword, pulled an enemy general off his horse and captured him with his bare hands. But brave as they were, not one of the three ever went near an oxcart again.

"A samurai does not fear death," they would say. "But some things are worse than death. An oxcart is one of them."

THE BATTLE OF CHIHAYA CASTLE

All samurai pledged loyalty to the emperor. The truth was, however, that throughout most of Japan's history the emperor was little more than a figurehead. The country's actual rulers were the leaders of powerful military clans who claimed to govern in the emperor's name. Only once did an emperor attempt to recover his rightful power. With the help of a courageous general, Kusunoki Masashige, he nearly succeeded.

THE GREAT commander Kusunoki Masashige was once besieged in Chihaya Castle by an army of his enemies, the Hojo clan. Kusunoki had only two hundred samurai within the walls. The Hojo army numbered several thousand, with more arriving each day.

Kusunoki grew deeply worried as the siege dragged on. The castle's food supply was diminishing. Soon there would be nothing to eat at all. None of the tricks or tactics he tried in order to break the siege had worked. The Hojo had lost dozens of soldiers in attacks and counterattacks; but they did not appear to mind.

Whenever a Hojo samurai fell, two more appeared to take his place.

After several weeks, Kusunoki had lost so many of his own soldiers that he could hardly defend the castle. Cooks, grooms, servants—anyone who could hold a weapon—was sent to fight on the ramparts. *If this siege goes on much longer, I will have to surrender*, he thought to himself one night as he sat alone in his room. A paper lantern threw shadows against the wall, shadows that seemed as dark as Kusunoki's fears for the future.

The brave commander knew that far more was at stake than just one castle. The Hojo had ruled Japan for generations. Having made the emperor their puppet, they did as they pleased. Hojo officials looted the treasury. Hojo judges demanded bribes. Hojo samurai took what they wanted. No one dared challenge them.

One brave emperor, Go-Daigo, tried to regain the power that was rightfully his by leading a revolt against the Hojo. It failed. Go-Daigo, now a prisoner, was sent to a remote island. His followers were scattered.

Only Kusunoki and his samurai fought on. He had made Chihaya Castle a rallying point for all who supported the emperor. If it fell the Hojo would rule unchallenged. Japan would never be free of their tyranny.

As Kusunoki pondered his few remaining choices, he heard a faint knock at the door. He opened it to find a little girl standing on the threshold, holding a sleeping baby in her arms.

"What do you want, child?" Kusunoki asked. "If your parents sent you to beg for food, tell them I have none to give. I am sorry you and your baby sister are hungry, but there is nothing I can do."

The little girl bowed. "My lord, you are mistaken. This is not my sister. This is my doll. My mother made her. Isn't she pretty?"

Kusunoki frowned. "I have more important things to worry about than dolls. Your mother knows the castle is under siege! Why did she send you to bother me?"

"My mother knows where you can find more soldiers. Won't you talk to her?"

Kusunoki got up, grumbling. "Very well. Take me to her. It cannot hurt to listen."

The child led Kusunoki to a large room overlooking the eastern wall. Moonlight streamed in through the narrow windows. Tatami mats and colorful pieces of cloth covered the floor where a dozen women sat together, sewing. The women rose and bowed when the commander entered.

"Thank you for coming, Lord Kusunoki," said the child's mother. "Ever since the siege began, the women of Chihaya Castle have met in this room. We keep up our courage by sewing. The more we stitch, the less time we have to worry about the battle outside. Our husbands tell us there are not enough soldiers to defend the castle walls. Without reinforcements, Chihaya will fall. We have been thinking about what we could do to help. We believe we have discovered a plan to save our castle."

"Let me hear it." Kusunoki sat down to listen.

Seven days passed. At dawn on the eighth day, the Hojo came out of their tents. They saw twenty-four samurai standing before the gates of Chihaya Castle in battle order.

"Kusunoki's men are coming out!" they cried to one another. "They realize the castle is doomed to fall. They want to die fighting. Hurry! We will give them the battle they seek!"

The leading samurai grabbed their weapons and ran charging toward the castle. Each wanted the honor of striking the enemy first.

Crouching on the battlements, Kusunoki waited for the attacking samurai to draw near. Suddenly he gave the signal. The few remaining defenders on the walls stood up. Their arrows decimated the astonished swordsmen. Within seconds, the bravest fighters in the Hojo army lay dead.

The Hojo generals were outraged. "Attack! Attack!" they shouted to their soldiers. The Hojo army came rushing across the field. The defenders' arrows swept their ranks, killing dozens with each volley.

The Hojo soldiers fought their way through the rain of arrows to the walls of the castle where twenty-four Chihaya samurai stood with weapons drawn, awaiting their attack.

The Hojo commander shouted, "Kill those treacherous rogues! They lured us into this trap!" The Hojo army fell upon the samurai, cutting them down, hacking them to pieces. Suddenly they stopped, embarrassed and confused.

"These samurai aren't men. They're dolls dressed in armor!"

Suddenly they heard laughter coming from the walls above. "Look at the brave Hojo!" one of Kusunoki's men called out. "They have conquered an army of dolls!"

"It takes a real dummy to overcome a dummy!" another shouted.

The Hojo were enraged. They stood beneath the wall, shaking their fists at the soldiers above.

"It's easy for cowards to laugh when they hide behind a wall. Come out of the castle!" they shouted back. "You won't be laughing long if you come down here!"

"We accept your challenge," Kusunoki called to the Hojo. "Prepare yourselves. We are coming out now!"

The Hojo gathered before the gate, ready to attack the moment it opened. Kusunoki gave another signal and immediately an avalanche of heavy stones, bricks, hot lead, and boiling water poured down on the Hojo from above. The assault took the Hojo by surprise. Dozens were killed. The rest fled back to their camp in disgrace.

There was no honor for those who died, and certainly none for those who ran away. Kusunoki Masashige had killed eight hundred Hojo fighters in that battle. His only loss was twenty-four dolls.

The Hojo were so humiliated by this defeat that they ended the siege and marched away.

"A long road lies ahead of us. There will be many more battles until our emperor is free and the Hojo are overthrown," Kusunoki told his followers at the victory feast. "Today we can rejoice, for we have given the Hojo a beating they won't soon forget, thanks to the cleverness and skill of the brave women of Chihaya Castle—and to the matchless courage of twenty-four samurai dolls."

TOMOE
GOZEN

The wives and daughters of samurai families were as courageous as the men. When enemies attacked Wakamatsu Castle, the women of the Aizu clan helped defend the walls. Twenty of them donned armor to fight beside their husbands and brothers. One, Nakano Takeko, charged the enemy with a naginata, *a Japanese pike, and cut down several men.*

Indeed, a woman of the Minamoto clan stands among the greatest samurai heroes of all time. This is her story.

Not all warriors were men. One of the most famous was a woman. Her name was Tomoe Gozen.

As a little girl Tomoe Gozen refused to learn the arts considered proper for a woman of her rank. She did not want to arrange flowers, or practice playing music on the koto or *biwa*. She wanted to become a samurai like her father and brothers.

One day Tomoe sneaked out of the house and ran to the dojo, where her brothers practiced the martial arts under the supervision of their *sensei*.

"Teach me, too!" Tomoe demanded.

"It is not proper for girls to study swordsmanship. Go back to your mother," the *sensei* told her.

"I won't! Not unless you promise to teach me something."

"Very well. Join your brothers. Do what they do."

The boys were practicing kata, a series of strenuous exercises. The *sensei* thought Tomoe would grow tired and go away. Instead, she persisted. When she practiced bare-handed fighting with the boys, she did not cry when she was knocked down. She got up, bowed to her opponent, and continued striking and kicking. The *sensei* noted that she scored some excellent points against boys who were bigger and far more experienced than she was.

When practice came to an end, Tomoe asked the *sensei*, "Well, did I prove myself worthy? May I come back?"

"I will have to speak to your father," the *sensei* replied.

———————

"My daughter wants to study the martial arts?" Tomoe Gozen's father asked in disbelief when the *sensei* told him how she had come to the dojo.

"It is not as far-fetched as you think," the *sensei* explained. "She is a descendant of a long line of samurai. The blood of warriors flows in her veins. Remember, in times past the women of our clan fought valiantly beside the men. Your daughter is following her ancient heritage. If you forbid her to study, she will become angry and bitter. Let her practice with the boys as long as she wishes. I do not mind having her in the dojo. She is a good student who works very hard. She sets a fine example for the others. The boys must do their best if they hope to keep up with her."

Tomoe's father allowed her to continue studying with the *sensei*.

By the time Tomoe Gozen was old enough to marry, she had mastered all the martial arts. She accompanied her father and brothers on military campaigns. Here she proved her skill again and again, riding into battle with reckless courage and striking down many renowned samurai.

Tomoe married her cousin Minamoto no Yoshinaka, a famous hero. She fought at his side against their family's enemies, the Taira clan. Tomoe's brother, Imai Kunehira, fought with them.

Yoshinaka defeated the Taira in many hard-fought battles. In one famous encounter, he drove the enemy into a narrow valley where they were ambushed by hidden soldiers. Seventy thousand Taira samurai lost their lives. The victorious Minamoto warriors hailed Yoshinaka and his wife, Tomoe Gozen, who had fought beside him.

Not all were pleased by the victory. Minamoto no Yoritomo, the clan's leader, became jealous of his cousin Yoshinaka. He decided to get rid of the brave young hero before he became too powerful to overthrow.

Yoritomo ordered his two brothers to attack Yoshinaka. The two Minamoto armies fought a bloody battle on the banks of the Uji river. Tomoe and her brother led charge after charge against their treacherous cousins.

As the battle raged, an enemy general named Uchida Iyeyoshi attempted to capture Tomoe. He grasped the sleeve of her robe and tried to pull her off her horse. Tomoe galloped off, leaving her sleeve in Iyeyoshi's hand. Iyeyoshi waved it like a banner for all to see.

"Look! I have beaten Tomoe Gozen! See what I have taken from her!"

Tomoe heard his boastful cry. Outraged, she charged at Iyeyoshi, dragging him from his horse and cutting off his head. She galloped along the battle line, holding the head high and crying, "Look! I have beaten Uchida Iyeyoshi! See what *I* have taken from *him*!"

Yet, all of Tomoe's courage could not change the battle's outcome. Yoshinaka's forces were outnumbered. No matter how many enemy soldiers they killed, more arrived to take their place. By the end of the day it was clear the battle was lost.

Yoshinaka's followers began to retreat, but Yoshinaka continued fighting. Tomoe Gozen and Imai Kunehira fought beside him. Their armor was feathered with arrows. They bled from many wounds. But they would not surrender or retreat.

Soon the brave trio were the only ones left of their army. The rest had all been captured or killed. The battle was lost.

Minamoto Yoshinaka said to Imai Kunehira, "It is too late to escape. We are surrounded. If we are captured, we will be tortured and put to death as traitors. Better for us to take our own lives and die with dignity."

Tomoe Gozen looked at her husband and brother for the last time. "I am not ready to give up. I will make my stand by the riverbank. Go quickly. I will hold off the enemy to give you time to end your lives honorably."

Tomoe Gozen hurled herself at Yoritomo's

forces as her husband and brother swam their horses across the river. They did not get far. Yoshinaka's horse became mired in quicksand. As the brave samurai struggled to get free, an arrow struck him in the face. Two enemy soldiers dragged the wounded leader from his horse and cut off his head. Imai Kunehira vowed not to be taken alive. He put the point of his sword in his mouth and leaped from the saddle. His sword was driven through his brain, and he died.

Still fighting, Tomoe Gozen heard the enemy begin to cheer. She looked across the river and saw soldiers carrying the heads of her husband and brother on spears. The enemy closed around her. But Tomoe would not be taken captive. She spurred her horse and charged through the battle line, striking down enemy samurai left and right. No one dared pursue her. She galloped over a ridge and disappeared.

Tomoe Gozen was never seen again. Minamoto no Yoritomo and his brothers said that she had been badly wounded in battle and probably crawled into a cave somewhere to die. Nobody believed them. If someone had seriously wounded Tomoe, he would have bragged about it. No one did.

It is possible that she committed sepukku, the ritual suicide ceremony by which defeated or disgraced samurai ended their lives. It is more likely, however, that she hung up her sword forever. Disgusted by her cousin's treachery, she withdrew from a world where people like Minamoto no Yoritomo ruled. And so, some believe, she became a Buddhist nun, spending the rest of her life doing good deeds, studying holy texts, and offering prayers every day for the souls of her husband and brother.

THE BURGLAR

What made the samurai such ferocious fighters? They were not afraid to die. From the time they were small boys, samurai were trained to be completely indifferent to death and suffering—their own as well as that of others. It was this fearlessness that allowed a single medieval swordsman to charge an entire army.

Such magnificent heroism has a dark side. Indifference to death allowed samurai to test their swords on the bodies of living criminals. The qualities that make a good soldier are not always the ones that make a good human being.

MINAMOTO NO YORINOBU was a distinguished samurai who fought in many battles. As a reward for his courage, the shogun appointed him governor of Kōzuke province. Yorinobu proved to be as outstanding a governor as he was a warrior. He was honest and hardworking. He judged everyone fairly, no matter what their rank. Despite these qualities, there was a coldness about him that frightened people. It was said: Yorinobu is not afraid to die. He is not afraid if anyone else dies, either.

Among Yorinobu's officers was a samurai named Fujiwara no Chikataka. Chikataka was a

brave man but unsteady. He was known for losing his temper in a crisis.

One night, when Chikataka was on duty at
the governor's palace, a burglar broke into his
house. The guards quickly discovered the desperate man. They chased him down the hallway
and into the family's sleeping quarters. The
noise awakened Chikataka's daughter, a beautiful girl of seventeen. She looked outside her
room to see what was happening. Trapped by
the guards, the burglar grabbed the girl.

"Come any closer and I'll kill her!" the man
shouted, pressing a dagger to her throat. Chikataka's wife and sons appeared on the scene.

"Harm our sister and we'll cut you to
pieces!" the boys cried, brandishing their
swords. Chikataka's wife began screaming. The
daughter added her own wails to the din as she
pleaded for her life. The guards bellowed orders
at each other. It was total confusion.

"Send for Lieutenant Chikataka!" someone
cried. Two of the guards ran off to fetch him.

Chikataka arrived, trembling with anger. He shouted at the burglar, "Release my daughter, you criminal! If you harm her in any way, I'll see you burned alive!"

"Back off or she dies!" the burglar shouted back.

By now the commotion had awakened the whole neighborhood. People came out of their houses in their nightclothes and gathered in the street. Word of the disturbance quickly reached the governor's palace. Yorinobu, awakened in the dead of night, came down to investigate. He ordered his guards to wait outside. Accompanied by one secretary, he entered Chikataka's house. The frightened servants quickly took him to the hallway where the burglar held the girl hostage.

"Be quiet, all of you!"

The shouting and screaming stopped.

"Bring me a stool," the governor said. As soon as one arrived, he sat down in the middle of the hallway. Yorinobu addressed the burglar. The crowd was silent.

"Tell me something. I want to know what this girl did to make you hate her enough to want to kill her."

"I don't hate her. She has done nothing to me," the burglar protested. "I don't even know her. I never saw her before tonight."

"If you don't want to kill her, why are you holding that knife to her throat?"

"I don't know what else to do! If I let her go, these people will cut me down. I'm only trying to save my life."

"Listen to me," the governor said calmly. "You have nothing to fear. If I can show you a way to save your life, will you let the girl go?"

The burglar nodded. "I will."

"Do exactly as I tell you. Hand me that dagger. As soon as you do, I want you to release the girl. I promise no harm will come to you."

The burglar hesitated. Could he trust the governor? He lowered his arm and handed the dagger to Yorinobu. Chikataka's daughter wrenched herself from his grasp and ran to her father.

"Kill him now!" Chikataka and his sons ran forward to attack the burglar. Yorinobu rose from his stool, the dagger in his hand.

"Stop! All of you! I promised this man his life if he freed the girl. Would you make me a liar? This burglar is under my protection. I'll defend him with my life. If you want to kill him, you'll have to kill me first."

Chikataka and his sons backed away. Yorinobu sat down again. He spoke to the frightened man.

"Our business is not finished. You still haven't explained why you broke into this house tonight."

"My lord, I was desperate. I did not know what else to do. My parents are farmers—good people who raised me well. I was lazy. I wanted no part of the hard labor that is the farmer's life. I came to the city to seek my fortune. Having no skills and little taste for work, I fell in with a gang of robbers. We broke into houses at night, stealing whatever we could find. It was easy. The people were asleep. We took what we wanted.

One night, a man awoke and challenged us. The leader of our band killed him. That was enough for me. I wanted no part of murder. When I told the others I wanted to leave the gang, they threatened to kill me. They said I knew too much. I had to leave the city, but I had no money, no place to go. I thought if I could commit just one more burglary, I could get enough money to make my escape and start a new life. That's why I came here. But as you see, everything went wrong from the beginning." The burglar hung his head in shame.

"That is a sad tale, but it may yet have a happy ending," Yorinobu said. "Tell me the names of the men in your gang and where they can be found."

The burglar confessed everything. The governor's secretary wrote it all down.

"I'll see that these men are rounded up and punished." Yorinobu turned to Chikataka. "Run to the palace. Bring back a fast horse, saddled and bridled, along with a sword and a bag filled with enough rice for ten days."

The lieutenant returned with everything the governor requested. "Mount up," Yorinobu told the burglar. As soon as the man was in the saddle, the governor gave him the sword, the rice, and a purse of money. "Ride as fast and as far as you can. Don't let anyone stop you. You have enough rice for ten days. Keep on until you come to a village where nobody knows who you are. Settle there. Use this money to start a new life, an honest one. Don't ever come back here. If I see you again, I'll have you cut to pieces."

As the burglar galloped away into the night, Chikataka exclaimed to the governor, "My lord, what an amazing achievement! You rescued my daughter, showed the burglar justice and mercy, broke up a gang of thieves—all without shedding blood or even drawing your sword! How did you accomplish that?"

"I'm disappointed with you, Chikataka," the governor said. "When are you going to learn to control your temper? There was no need to wake up the whole city in the middle of the night. You could have accomplished as much as I did, if only you'd remained calm."

"My lord, how can you expect me to be calm with a burglar holding a knife to my daughter's throat? He could have killed her at any moment!"

"Which is precisely why you must maintain self-control. As boys we samurai are taught to overcome our fear of death. Most never fully understand what that means. A samurai like yourself, Chikataka, may be able to die in a dozen terrible ways without flinching. You may walk over the corpses of your dearest friends with complete indifference. But when your wife or children are threatened, you fall to pieces. That is a serious weakness.

"Human life must mean nothing to us, Chikataka, especially the lives of those we love best. You were terrified that your daughter might be killed, which is why you could do nothing to help her. I, on the other hand, did not care if she lived or died. I would have felt the same if that burglar were holding his knife to my own daughter's throat. Consequently, I could study the situation without fear or anger clouding my thoughts, and save her life."

Chikataka trembled. "This is not the way of a father."

"It is the way of the warrior," Yorinobu answered.

DEVIL BOY

Japan's seemingly endless wars brought glory to the samurai but only hardship and misery to the common people, who had to pay for them with taxes and see their brothers, fathers, and sons drafted as common soldiers. When the burden became too great, many farmers rebelled, taking to the hills, where they often defeated the armies sent against them. To the powerful rulers these rebels were bandits. To the ordinary farmers they were heroes.

LORD RAIKŌ once visited his brother, Minamoto no Yorinobu, at his country estate. His four favorite samurai accompanied him. Their names were Tsuna, Kintoki, Sadamitsu, and Suetake.

When they arrived in the courtyard, they saw a powerful-looking young man tied to a stake with only a thin cord. His shoulders were as broad as an ox yoke, suggesting enormous strength.

"Who is that fellow?" Lord Raikō asked his brother. "Why is he tied up like that?"

"Oho!" Lord Yorinobu exclaimed. "That's Kidōmaru—Devil Boy—the famous outlaw! We've been trying to catch him for years. This time we were lucky. We found him sleeping in a cave. I lit a fire at the entrance and smoked him out, but in trying to escape he killed seven of my best fighters. Finally the priests at the temple gave us a magic cord. That was the only way we could bind him.

"So you're the notorious Devil Boy," Lord Raikō said to the young man. "What do you have to say for yourself?"

The outlaw glared at Lord Raikō. "If one of my own men hadn't revealed my hiding place, you never would have captured me. Call me a bandit, if you like. To the farmers of this district, I'm a hero. *You're* the bandits. You take our crops and animals. You kidnap our sons and brothers to fight your meaningless wars. I hate all samurai. I've killed dozens of them!"

Lord Raikō turned to his brother. "Listen, Yorinobu. If I had a fellow like that as my prisoner, I wouldn't rely just on a magic cord to hold him. I'd bind him with chains and lock him in an iron cage, as well, to make sure he didn't get away."

"You're right. I shouldn't take chances," Lord Yorinobu said. He gave an order to his guards.

"You will pay for this!" Devil Boy screamed at Lord Raikō. "I'll be revenged, and sooner than you think!"

Lord Raikō laughed at him. "How dare you threaten me! You're nothing but a common farmer yourself. You belong in a cage like an animal. By tomorrow your head will be stuck on a pole and your body will feed the crows." He slapped Devil Boy across the face, then turned to join his brother for dinner.

That night while the household feasted, Yorinobu's guards wrapped Devil Boy with chains and thrust him into an iron cage. They were surprised that the outlaw did not resist. He sat in a corner of the cage with his face pressed against his knees. He seemed to have given up all hope.

After everyone had gone to bed, the guard brought him a bowl of rice. "It's your last meal. I hope you enjoy it."

"How can I eat, chained up like this?" Devil Boy asked.

"I'll come in and feed you if you promise you won't try to escape," the guard said. Devil Boy nodded. The guard unlocked the cage door. He came in, put down his sword, and began feeding Devil Boy clumps of rice with his *hashi* sticks.

"This rice is good. It gives me strength." Suddenly Devil Boy stood up. He flexed his muscles—and the iron chain shattered. The magic cord had had the power to restrain him, but when Lord Yorinobu showed lack of faith by doubting its power, the cord lost its strength. Devil Boy knew this. He strangled the astonished guard before he could cry out. Devil Boy laughed as he finished the rice and took the guard's sword.

"I promised I wouldn't try to escape, but I didn't promise not to kill you," he said as he left the cage. "Now it's Lord Raikō's turn."

Creeping through the shadows, Devil Boy

made his way to the manor house. He crouched beneath the window, expecting to hear Lord Raikō snoring. Instead, he overheard the lord telling his samurai, "Put on your armor. Make sure your swords are ready. We'll saddle the horses and leave tonight. I want to reach Mount Kurama by tomorrow afternoon."

"Why don't we wait until morning?" Sadamitsu asked. "It's raining, and still dark outside. Mount Kurama is not far away. We can easily get there by the afternoon."

"Listen to me and don't argue," Lord Raikō insisted. "There's something about this house I don't like. I sense danger here. The sooner we leave, the better."

The four samurai obeyed. They tied on their swords and armor, saddled their horses, and rode away with Lord Raikō in the night without even saying farewell to Lord Yorinobu.

Devil Boy, skulking in the shadows, was furious. His plan to murder Lord Raikō while he slept had failed. He was not so foolhardy as to attack five armed warriors when they were ready for him. Instead, he hurried down the Kurama road to prepare an ambush.

Devil Boy arrived at his chosen spot at dawn. The road wound through a deep ravine, where high walls permitted no escape. He cut large branches from trees, held them in both hands, and stood beside the road, perfectly still. From a distance he resembled a small stunted tree growing among the rocks. *I will stand here until Lord Raikō and his samurai approach,* he thought. *Then I will attack!*

The sky cleared as the sun came up. Lord Raikō, riding with his samurai, still felt a sense of danger. "Be alert," he told them as the road wound through a ravine. "This is a good place for an ambush."

"Let's shoot some arrows," Suetake suggested. "If anyone's lurking among those trees, they'll see that we're ready for them." He pointed to a stunted tree a hundred yards away. "Tsuna, I challenge you to hit that!"

"Nothing is easier!" Tsuna drew back his bowstring and shot an arrow into the tree. "You try, Kintoki."

One after another, Tsuna, Kintoki, Sadamitsu, and Suetake took turns shooting arrows at the tree.

It was no tree at all, but Devil Boy, standing beside the road, camouflaging himself with branches. So great was his courage and desire for revenge that he never moved, even as one arrow after another struck him.

The samurai came closer, laughing and joking with one another. Suddenly Devil Boy threw down the branches. Bristling with arrows, he let out a terrifying scream as he drew his sword and charged at Lord Raikō. Tsuna blocked the charge with his horse. Devil Boy swept him from the saddle with one stroke. He wheeled and dealt Suetake a mighty blow that shattered the samurai's helmet and sent blood pouring down his face. Sadamitsu and Kintoki attacked together. Kintoki went down with a cut to the leg as Devil Boy slashed at Sadamitsu, wounding him in the side. He would have killed them both if Lord Raikō had not ridden up behind Devil Boy and cut off his head.

Even with his head gone, Devil Boy kept fighting! His body continued swinging the sword, spouting blood from its neck until it collapsed. The head bounced up from the ground and bit Lord Raikō on the thigh. Finally Devil Boy died.

As the samurai bound up their wounds, Lord Raikō said to his companions, "He was a wicked bandit, but what a courageous fighter! If he hadn't been weakened by our arrows, he would have killed us all."

They wrapped Devil Boy's body and head in a blanket, which they carried back to Lord Yorinobu, who gave him a hero's funeral.

THE *RŌNIN* AND THE TEA MASTER

Chanoyu, *the Japanese tea ceremony, was inspired by the teachings of Zen Buddhism. As the tea master prepares and serves the tea, he empties his mind of all thoughts and cares, concentrating only on the moment. This deep concentration produces a sense of great peace. Chanoyu follows a complex ritual. Only a few have ever thoroughly mastered it. Today, in the hustle and bustle of modern Japan, thousands of people still make time in their busy lives to practice the tea ceremony. Tea masters are regarded as living national treasures.*

Rōnin *were at the opposite end of the scale. These unemployed samurai are often depicted as bullies and bandits. Fighting was all they knew. When the wars ended and the armies disbanded, they had no way of earning a living. Many became outlaws, preying on the society that had cast them out.*

A GREAT LORD and his household once traveled to the mountains to visit a certain temple. A famous tea master went with them. The lord was devoted to the art of the tea ceremony and practiced it every day with the help of the tea master, his instructor. The lord was very fond of his teacher. To show his esteem, the lord allowed the tea master to wear his *mon*— the ornamental crest worn by all the lord's retainers. The tea master was also entitled to carry a sword as a special badge of honor.

While in the mountains, the tea master went off alone to view a certain shrine. Suddenly a *rōnin* jumped out from behind a tree.

"Ah! You carry a sword. You must be a samurai. Show me your skill. Let us fight!" cried the *rōnin*. Of course, the *rōnin* knew the tea master carried the sword only as a courtesy and had no idea how to use it. The *rōnin* didn't really expect the tea master to fight. He hoped to frighten him into giving up money or something of value in exchange for his life.

The tea master would have done that—had he not been wearing a *mon*. To bear a lord's crest is to carry his honor. If the tea master behaved like a coward, it would reflect on his lord.

"You are mistaken. I am no samurai. I know nothing of the art of swordsmanship," the tea master replied. "However, I will not dishonor my lord, whose crest I wear. I accept your challenge. All I ask is that you allow me a few hours to prepare myself."

The *rōnin* laughed as he sheathed his sword. "Agreed! We will meet here at noon and fight to the finish."

The tea master walked back toward the temple, thinking hard about what to do. He was not afraid to die, but he did not want to look foolish in the way he handled a sword. Then he remembered having passed a dojo on his way to the shrine. He stopped here and asked to speak to the *sensei*.

"What can I do for you?" the *sensei* asked.

The tea master replied, "I would like you to teach me how to die."

The *sensei* chuckled. "That is an unusual request. Most of my students come to me because they want to live."

"I am a special case," the tea master said. He went on to tell the *sensei* about his encounter with the *rōnin* and how he had agreed to meet with him in a few hours to fight to the death.

"I see," said the *sensei*, more serious now. "The art of the sword is like the art of the tea ceremony. Both take a lifetime to learn. Neither can be mastered in a few hours. However, allow me to show you the beginning position."

The *sensei* showed the tea master how to place his feet, how to hold his sword, and how to assume the correct posture for beginning a duel.

The tea master practiced these exercises for a while.

"Good," said the *sensei*. "Now put away your sword. I would like you to do something else." The *sensei* clapped his hands. One of his students carried in a tray. On it were arranged all the bowls and utensils needed for the tea ceremony. "I, too, am devoted to the tea ceremony, though my skill in the art is poor compared to your own," the *sensei* began. "Would you honor my students and myself by performing the ceremony for us?"

"With the greatest pleasure," said the tea master. As he arranged the utensils in their proper places, he thought, *This may be the last time I will ever perform the tea ceremony. Let me strive to make it the best.* He cleared his mind of all unnecessary thoughts and emotions, focusing all his concentration on each separate action as the ceremony unfolded.

The tea ceremony came to an end. The *sensei* sighed. "Ah, that was beautiful! I have never seen the tea ceremony performed so exquisitely.

You truly are a master of the art. I do not know if it is possible for a human being to achieve perfection in such things, but I believe you have come as close to it as any mortal ever has. Now I have something to tell you."

The tea master listened carefully.

"When you meet the *rōnin*, draw your sword and assume the first position, just as I showed you. Close your eyes, and in your mind go through all the steps of the tea ceremony, just as you have performed it now. When you hear the *rōnin* shout, strike down with your sword as hard as you can."

"What will that accomplish?" the tea master asked.

"Probably nothing," said the *sensei*. "Most likely he will kill you. But you will have died fighting, executing a precise, swordsmanlike move. You will have a samurai's death. Neither you nor your lord will be dishonored."

The tea master thanked the *sensei*. Then he set out to meet the *rōnin*.

He found the *rōnin* waiting for him by the

tree. "Well, Master Samurai, are you prepared to fight?" the *rōnin* jeered.

"I am," the tea master said. He assumed the first position, drew his sword, and raised it above his head. Clearing away all thoughts of hope and fear, he began the tea ceremony in his mind with such intense concentration that he could see the bowls and utensils arranged before him.

The ceremony came to an end, but the tea master had still not heard the *rōnin* shout. He opened his eyes—and saw the *rōnin* in the distance, running away down the path. The outlaw's sword lay beneath the tree, where he had thrown it.

Puzzled, the tea master picked up the *rōnin*'s sword and brought it back to the *sensei*. "What does this mean?" he asked.

The *sensei* congratulated the tea master with great joy. "I will explain everything to you. When you first came to me, I told you that the art of the sword was much like the art of the tea ceremony. So it is. As we practice each art, we strive to attain an inner stillness—a concentration so intense that it allows us to act without thinking. Once we have achieved that state, we no longer perform the art. It performs itself through us."

"I understand," said the tea master. "But why did the *rōnin* run away instead of attacking me?"

"When you performed the tea ceremony in your mind, the expression of concentration on your face was one that only the greatest masters of the sword ever achieve. When the *rōnin* saw that expression, he became frightened. He did not know if you knew anything about swordsmanship; but if you did, he could not hope to stand against you. His courage left him, and, coward that he was, he threw down his sword and ran away."

The tea master thanked the *sensei* and returned to his lord, having not only saved his life and honor but also having learned a great lesson. For just as a great tree has many roots, so does a wise man have many teachers.

NO SWORD

Surprising as it may seem, most of the great samurai masters were nonviolent men at heart. They fought bravely when challenged or when their lords summoned them to battle. If they had had their choice, however, the majority would have preferred to write poetry, contemplate the beauty of nature, draw, paint, listen to music, or meditate. They longed for the day when their country would be at peace and the martial arts would be practiced only in the dojo, not on the battlefield.

TSUKAHARA BOKUDEN was one of the most famous swordsmen in Japanese history, and one of the few to die of old age.

Bokuden lived during a time of civil war, when rival clans fought one another to control the country. Bokuden saw his sons and many of his most beloved students perish in battle. Sickened by the endless violence, he gradually changed his views about swordsmanship. Bokuden founded a new school of the martial arts. He taught his students that samurai should try to achieve victory with a minimum of violence and the least amount of bloodshed—preferably without even drawing their swords. He called his new school Mutekatsu Ryu, which means "to defeat the enemy without hands." In other words, no sword.

Bokuden once took a ferry across Lake Biwa. Among the passengers was another samurai, a loud, arrogant fellow who was looking for a fight. This samurai pushed and insulted the other passengers. Stepping in front of Bokuden, he sneered, "You look like you might know something of swordsmanship. Are you really a samurai, or just an actor dressed up as one?"

Bokuden ignored the insult. "I am a samurai. And I may know a little of the swordsman's art. I have studied it most of my life."

"What school do you belong to?" the braggart asked.

"I have my own school. It differs from others. I call it Mutekatsu Ryu, the 'no-sword' school," Bokuden told him.

"No sword? What does that mean?"

"It means that achieving your goal is more important than overcoming your opponent. I teach my students to use their wits instead of force. A student of my school will always try to win without violence whenever possible. Preferably without even drawing his sword."

The samurai laughed. "What nonsense is this! That sounds like a coward's way to me. I would like to see this no-sword school of yours in action."

"I am happy to oblige." Bokuden told the ferryman to steer to a nearby island.

The samurai jumped off the boat. He stood with his sword raised, prepared to receive an attack. "Now, show me this no-sword school!"

"Here it is," said Bokuden. He took the ferryman's pole and pushed the boat away from the island, leaving the samurai stranded on shore.

"See!" said Bokuden, as the ferry rowed away. "No sword."

A Glossary of Samurai Terms

biwa (BEE-wah): a musical stringed instrument; a Japanese lute.

Bushido (BOO-shi-do): the samurai code of conduct. The word means "way of the warrior," as translated from Japanese.

chanoyu (CHA-no-yoo): the Japanese tea ceremony. A complex ritual for brewing and serving tea. It is both an art and a form of meditation.

dojo (DOH-jo): a school where the martial arts are taught.

hashi (HAH-she): Japanese term for chopsticks.

kata (KAH-tah): a combination of positions and movements performed as a physical and mental exercise.

koto (KOH-to): a musical stringed instrument; a Japanese dulcimer.

Kyoto (KYOH-toh): Japan's official capital from A.D. 794 until 1869. Kyoto was the nation's cultural, religious, and artistic center for over a thousand years. The emperor resided in Kyoto.

mon (MONE): family crest.

naginata (NAH-gin-AH-ta): a long pole fitted with a curved blade on one end; a Japanese pike.

rōnin (ROH-nin): a masterless samurai. The Japanese word is translated as "wave person."

samurai (SAH-muh-rye): the Japanese warrior caste. A soldier or knight in the service of a powerful lord or clan leader. The Japanese word is translated as "one who serves."

sensei (SEN-say): a teacher of the martial arts.

seppuku (SEH-poo-koo): a form of ritual suicide unique to samurai. People committing seppuku would end their lives by stabbing themselves in the stomach with a dagger. Samurai might commit seppuku if they felt disgraced or if their honor had been called into question. They might also end their lives to call attention to an injustice. Finally, a lord might order a samurai to commit seppuku as punishment for a crime or serious error. The Japanese word is translated as "opening the belly."

shogun (SHO-gun): a prominent general or clan leader who held real political power. Although the emperor was highly respected, the shogun was the nation's actual ruler. The word *shogun* comes from a Chinese term translated as "barbarian-subduing great general."

taiko (TIE-ko): large ceremonial drums beaten during festivals.

Source Notes

In March 1997, I was invited to Japan to speak to children at the American schools in Tokyo and Osaka. My wife and I also spent one magical day in Kyoto, visiting the temples and gardens. My experiences during those memorable two and a half weeks inspired me to create a collection of Japanese stories.

When I began collecting samurai tales, I was surprised by how different they were from what I had expected. My notions about the samurai were largely derived from Akira Kurosawa movies. Many, of course, were exciting tales of duels and battles. But I found just as many stories that were deeply spiritual, romantic, and even nonviolent. Some were downright funny. The samurai enjoyed a joke and weren't too proud to laugh at themselves.

"Matajuro's Training," "Tomoe Gozen," "The Battle of Chihaya Castle," "The *Rōnin* and the Tea Master," and "No Sword" are based on factual accounts recorded in Harry Cook's *Samurai: The Story of a Warrior Tradition* (New York: Sterling Publishing Company, 1993).

Other versions of "The Oxcart," "Devil Boy," "The Burglar," and "The Coward" can be found in Hiroaki Sato's *Legends of the Samurai* (New York: Overlook Press, 1995), which draws from the original histories, documents, poetry, and literature of the samurai period.

"Dōhaku's Head" is adapted from Yamamoto Tsunetomo's classic work *Hagakure: The Book of the Samurai,* written in 1716 and translated by William Scott Wilson (Tokyo: Kodansha Press, 1987).

A version of "The Samurai and the Dragon," called "The Unlucky Warrior," can be found on several Internet sites that list folktales from around the world. No source or author is given on any of these sites, and I have been unable to track down a Japanese source for the story. The origins of this tale remain uncertain.

A NOTE ON JAPANESE NAMES

Names and titles from the samurai period can be extremely complex. Generally, the clan or family name comes before the personal name. Minamoto no Yoshinaka, for example, would be translated as "Yoshinaka of the Minamoto clan." However, famous samurai were known by various names at different times of their lives. They might change their names by acquiring new titles or positions, by winning important victories, or by undergoing life-changing experiences. The names of the individuals used in these stories are those by which they were identified in the sources. The suffix "-san" is added to a person's first name as a polite form of direct address in Japanese.